DR. ROACH'S MONSTROUS STORIES

FROGOSAURUS VS. THE BOG MONSTER

SCHOLASTIC INC.

Contents

Dr. Roach Welcomes YOU!

Do you have a favorite place? Sammy and Tammy do. They love the quiet Boggy Marshes near their home.

Meet Maximus Sneer. An evil man with lots of money and a secret plan. He is going to drain the Boggy Marshes dry, then build houses, stores, and parking lots.

But instead of creating homes, he creates two giant monsters — without even knowing it.

How you ask? Come closer, my friend, and I'll tell you all about it.

Welcome to Dr. Roach's Monstrous Stories. Enjoy!

Dr. Roach

Chapter 1
Stinky Bog

Sammy Linnet stretched out his fishing net over the stinky, brown waters of the Boggy Marshes.

"Give me your hand," said Sammy to his twin sister, Tammy, "then I can reach that deep pool."

"Careful," said Tammy, grabbing him as he leaned out.

"Almost there," said Sammy. "Just a little bit farther . . ."

"HEY YOU!" The man's voice was a shock. Tammy screamed and let go of her brother's hand. Sammy hovered in

midair, waving his arms like windmills as he tried to stay balanced — then toppled face-first into the bog with a gloopy SPLURCH!

"Euurrggghhh," said Tammy, as Sammy struggled to get up, all covered in mud and slime. "You look like a bog monster!"

"Oh, very funny. Now help me out," Sammy replied.

"Not a chance — that mud stinks!" said Tammy, taking a step backward.

"Hey, you two!"

An angry man was standing behind them. He was the size and shape of a bear, but in this case the bear was wearing a bright yellow parka with SECURITY written on the back.

"What are you two doing?" he asked.

"We're collecting samples for our school science project," said Tammy. "There are lots of really rare animals and plants living here and . . ."

"Yeah? Well, not for much longer. This is private property now," said the man.

"Private property?" spluttered Sammy. "Since when?"

"Since Maximus Sneer bought it. Now clear out!"

Tammy and Sammy walked and squelched their way home, past men building a high fence around the Boggy Marshes.

"What does Maximus Sneer want with the Boggy Marshes?" said Tammy.

"I don't know, but

they've always been open to the public. He can't just fence them off!" said Sammy.

"You're right," Tammy agreed. "We should organize a protest or something."

"Great idea! Let's do it now," Sammy said.

"No," Tammy replied, holding her nose, "let's do it after you've had a bath."

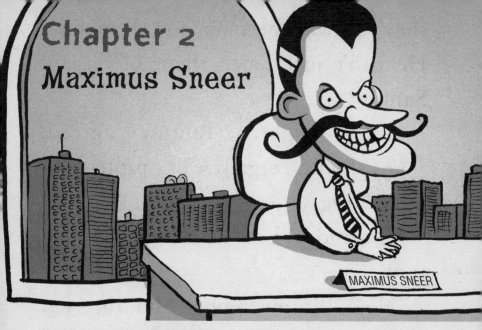

Chapter 2
Maximus Sneer

Maximus Sneer sat behind a large desk in his headquarters. In front of him, a large screen on the wall was showing plans for new buildings on the Boggy Marshes. A knock at the door disturbed Sneer's thoughts.

"Come in!" barked Sneer. "Perkins, it's you. What news do you have?"

"The draining work has started, Mr. Sneer," Perkins replied.

"And the water is being pumped into the Old Quarry?" Sneer asked.

"Yes, sir — just as you ordered," replied the man.

"Excellent, Perkins, excellent!"

"If I may be so bold, sir, don't we need permission to drain the marshes?" Perkins asked.

"Maximus Sneer does not ask permission for anything!" snapped Sneer.

9

He slammed his fist on a large button and the huge screen rose, revealing a large window that flooded the room with daylight. The window offered a view of the Boggy Marshes.

"Look at that, Perkins. Those marshes are nothing but mud and water! But soon they will be houses, stores, movie theaters, and parking lots. And they will all be mine!

And when people live there . . . they'll
be mine. And then I shall take over
the world!"

"The world, sir?" asked Perkins.

"Did I say world?" Sneer replied.

"Yes, sir, you did."

Across town, Sammy and Tammy were putting the finishing touches on their protest plans.

"So what do you think?" asked Tammy, holding up signs with the words SAVE OUR BOG painted on them.

"Great!" replied Sammy. "And I've put up posters telling people what's going on. There should be a good crowd for tomorrow's protest!"

"Yeah, let's hope so — we need something big to get Sneer's attention," said Tammy.

They were certainly going to get it.

Chapter 3
It's ALIVE!

The water from Sneer's pumps gushed into the Old Quarry and trickled down through the rocks. Then *drip, drip, drip* it went, into an underground cave and onto a large dried-up lump in the middle. The lump soaked up the water like a sponge until something remarkable happened. It opened its eyes.

Frogosaurus was ALIVE!

Who knows how long Frogosaurus had been trapped in the cave? A long time, that's for sure. It blinked its big, bulgy eyes and looked around. With a dry cracking sound, it opened its mouth and a long, pink tongue stretched out to catch the drips of water. Slowly, it stretched its froggy back legs and flexed its armlike front legs and gave itself a shake. Then Frogosaurus took a deep breath and, for the first time in thousands of years, gave its fearsome roar once again:

"Ribbit."

Frogosaurus gave a cough and tried again. This time it was thunderous.

"RRRRIIIIIIIBBBBBBBBBBIIIIIIIIIITTTTTTTTT!"

Meanwhile, back in Sneer's head-quarters, Maximus Sneer looked up from his smart phone.

"Perkins, did you hear something just then?" he asked.

"No, sir," Perkins replied.

"Hmm, strange," said Sneer, returning to his master plan, "very strange."

In the Boggy Marshes, the disappearing water was leaving thick, gloopy mud. The mud squished together and made lumps and bumps. The lumps and bumps became clumps, then heaps and mounds, and slowly squished themselves together to form a big slimy

mass. For the second time that day, something remarkable happened —

the mound of mud opened its eyes.

The mound began to move and a wobbly tower of mud rose into the air, slime slipping from the surface as it swayed from side to side. Two great muddy limbs appeared, followed by two great legs.

It saw the water draining away.

The Bog Monster thought of revenge!

Chapter 4
The Bog Monster Cometh!

Maximus Sneer sat scowling in the back seat of his luxury car.

"What on earth is taking so long, Perkins?" he barked at the driver.

"I'm sorry, Mr. Sneer, sir, but there seems to be some kind of demonstration up ahead," Perkins replied. "They're blocking the way into the marshes."

Sneer peered through the window. He could see a group of people waving signs and chanting.

"Pull over, Perkins! I'll deal with this!" shouted Sneer.

"Now, what is the meaning of this?" he barked as he flung open the door. "Who is in charge here?"

"We are," said Tammy and Sammy.

"Very amusing, now who's really in charge?" said Sneer.

"We are," said the twins again. "And we want you to leave the Boggy Marshes alone."

"Oh, this is priceless!" said Sneer, a thin smile splitting his wicked face. "Two junior mud huggers. Well, let me tell you,

Tweedle Dee and Tweedle Dum, or whatever your names are: You can't stop me because I represent business and you are children."

He spat out the last word like it tasted terrible.

"But we're not moving!" cried Tammy. "These marshes are special — they are home to loads of different plants and animals."

"Mr. Sneer, sir," said Perkins.

"Oh, please," said Sneer. "It's full of mud, slugs, and weeds. Name just one amazing thing that comes from that bog."

"Mr. Sneer, sir," repeated Perkins anxiously. "Look!"

In the distance was a great swaying tower of mud, twenty stories high, slowly slurping across the ground.

For a couple of seconds the crowd watched,

amazed, as the Bog Monster squelched toward them.

"It's going to get us!" someone shouted. Screaming, the crowd ran off in panic — even the police officers.

"Perkins!" Sneer cried. "Get me out of here! *Now!*"

RIALTO

NIGHT OF THE ZOMBIE GOLDFISH

Chapter 5
Frogosaurus Arrives

Maximus Sneer dived into his car and, with a squeal of tires, was gone. Only Tammy and Sammy were left.

"What's that?" exclaimed Sammy.

"I don't know — it looks like the bog has gotten up and moved," replied Tammy.

"Yeah — and we'd better do the same," said Sammy.

"Hold on a minute – what's that sound?" said Tammy, grabbing her brother's arm. There was a noise like someone speaking, but from a long way away.

"It's the police radio," said Sammy. She pointed to the squad car, which had been left when the police ran off. The radio was repeating a message.

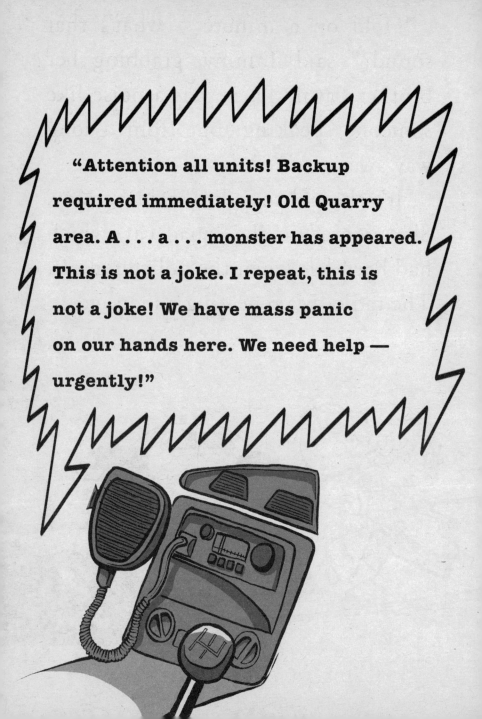

"Attention all units! Backup required immediately! Old Quarry area. A . . . a . . . monster has appeared. This is not a joke. I repeat, this is not a joke! We have mass panic on our hands here. We need help — urgently!"

"The Old Quarry? That's miles away!" said Tammy.

"So there are two monsters now?" said Sammy. "This I've got to see — let's go!"

In between the Boggy Marshes and the Old Quarry were Maximus Sneer's headquarters. Sneer's car squealed to a halt outside.

"Quick, Perkins," said Sneer as he got out of the car. "I want you to get

the police on the phone —
no, the army —
and make sure
that monster is
dealt with. It's
going to ruin
my plans!"

"And what would you like me to do
about THAT?" asked Perkins, pointing

behind Sneer.
His face was
white with fear.
"What are you
blathering about?"
snapped Sneer.
Then he saw
what Perkins
could see —

FROGOSAURUS!

A huge half-frog, half-human thing with giant bug eyes and a flicking tongue was leaping across the ground in gigantic bounds, straight toward them.

"Perkins!" cried Sneer. "Get me my mommy!"

Chapter 6
Mud Fight

Thirty seconds later, the Bog Monster arrived. And it spotted Frogosaurus. It was hate at first sight — there was room for only one monster here, and neither was going to back down.

Frogosaurus leaped at the Bog Monster in one massive bound and slammed into it with a huge SQUELCH!

The Bog Monster instantly changed shape and became a giant hand that swatted Frogosaurus aside with a soggy slap. The giant frog beast was sent tumbling backward — right into Maximus Sneer's headquarters. The Bog Monster built itself into a huge wave of mud and crashed into the building after Frogosaurus.

The next moment, Frogosaurus had leaped through the roof in an explosion of bricks, chairs, tables, and potted plants. It twisted in midair and landed back on top of the Bog Monster in another wild attack, mud flying everywhere. Frogosaurus bounded from

side to side, grabbing with its wiry arms and stabbing with its flicking tongue. The Bog Monster constantly changed shape trying to catch it.

A line of police officers outside the building kept the crowd of onlookers — including Tammy and Sammy — at a safe distance.

"Perkins, I demand that you do something!" shouted Sneer hysterically. He and Perkins were now so completely

covered in dirt that they looked like snowmen made of mud. "I will do something," Perkins replied. "I'm going to quit!"

And with that he walked off. Sneer turned to the police officers.

"Stop them! They're destroying my lovely building," Sneer whined.

"I'm afraid there's not much we can do," a police sergeant explained. "Typical! If you want something done, you've got to do it yourself!" snapped Sneer. He grabbed a megaphone from one of the officers.

"You two!" Sneer shouted at the monsters. "You are trespassing on my property! Leave now!"

The monsters stopped mid-fight and slowly turned to look at Sneer. Evil grins split their faces and they started to move toward him.

"Oh, dear . . ." whispered Sneer. "Mommy . . ."

Chapter 7
Brainstorm

As soon as the monsters changed direction, the crowd scattered. In one giant bound, Frogosaurus was among them, the Bog Monster sloshing up behind. People were screaming and panicking,

dashing this way and that. Fortunately the two monsters had difficulty choosing who to chase, and the people were too small to grab easily. Cars got squashed and buildings got smashed as Frogosaurus and the Bog Monster went on the rampage.

"We've got to do something," shouted Tammy.

"But what?" said Sammy.

"I've got an idea," Tammy replied. "They're from the marshes, right? Think about our science project — what's bad for the marshes?"

"Um, too much heat or water can

kill off a lot of the life that's there," said Sammy.

"And that's exactly what we've got to give the monsters," said Tammy. "We give the gloopy one so much water that it makes it too weak to pull itself together. The other one looks drier, so we should try to dry it out completely."

"You're a genius!" said Sammy.

"I know," Tammy replied. "Now, let's get started."

The twins quickly explained their idea to the police sergeant and the plan swung into action.

Frogosaurus bounded into the town square. There were people all around the edges and, oddly, they all had barbecues. Frogosaurus didn't care.

It licked its lips and decided who to snatch first. It was beginning to feel uncomfortably warm, but there were so many people to chase that Frogosaurus ignored the heat.

It stretched out an arm and there was a terrible CRACK!

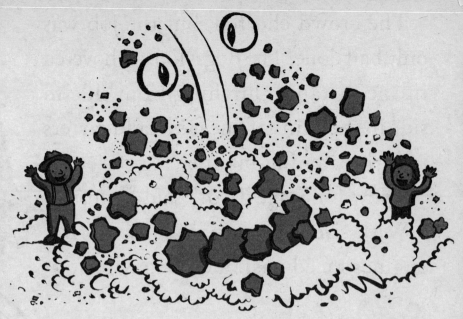

Frogosaurus was drying out — it needed water and fast. It stumbled around the square looking for an escape route. There was none. There were barbecues everywhere. Finally it tried to leap over the ring of fire, but its legs had dried out and lost their spring. Instead, it crashed to the ground — shattering into thousands of dry, crusty pieces.

The crowd cheered, but the job was only half done. The Bog Monster hovered in the distance, lurching from side to side in the ruins of Sneer's headquarters in a threatening manner.

"Now for Stage Two!" said Sammy.

With sirens blaring, the town's fire engines raced past. The Bog Monster

looked confused and
distracted by the noise and lights.
It did the only thing it could think
of — attack! It rose up high like a
giant wave of mud, ready to crash
down on the fire engines below. But
the water from the hoses hit the Bog
Monster first, sending it wheeling

backward. It tried swatting the water away but with no luck.

A huge pool of dirt began to form around the bottom of the Bog Monster, who swayed this way and that trying to avoid the high-powered jets.

Slowly, the flailing monster got smaller and the puddle got bigger, seeping and spreading across the ground, flooding the ruined building. With one last desperate attack, the Bog Monster hurled itself at the fire engines, but

splattered on the ground in a shower
of mud a good ways short of its
target.

The monsters were no more.

Tammy and Sammy reached the
ruined headquarters just as the Bog
Monster came to his gloopy end.

"So that's that," said Tammy.

Suddenly a small mound of mud rose from the ground. A quick blast from a hose sent it flying backward.

"Stop! Stop!" spluttered Maximus Sneer. "It's me!"

He stood sad and soggy among the boggy wasteland that had been his headquarters.

"You've learned a valuable lesson today, Mr. Sneer," said Sammy.

"What's that? Don't mess with nature?" Sneer replied.

"No," said Sammy. "If you're going to have a barbecue, always have some water close at hand, just in case."

The only person who didn't laugh was Maximus Sneer.

HURRY!

What can make all the mice in a small town suddenly stand still?

A giant piece of cheese? A huge mousetrap? No — a flying saucer from outer space!

Alien cats have come to Earth. These friendly felines say they come in peace, to help rid Buffalo Bottom of its mouse problem.

But when the town's cows start disappearing, Jilly McAfferty begins to worry. She thinks the visitors may be up to no good. Now she just has to prove it.

How you ask? Get a copy today and I'll tell you everything!

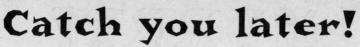

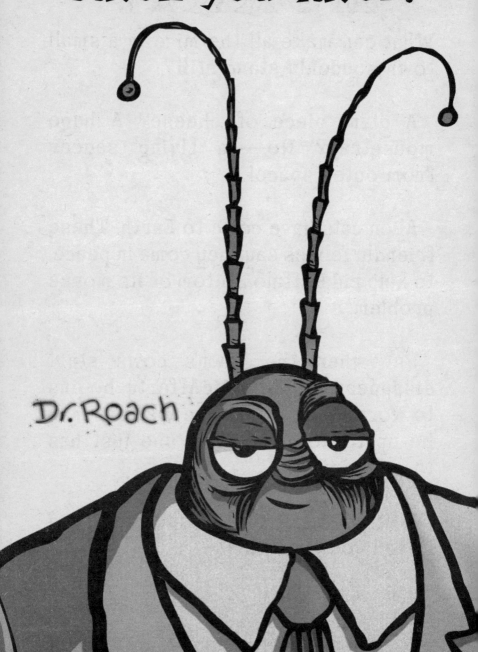